HORACE THE KING

THE JOURNEY

BOOK ONE

A N D Y H . N I L E S

Horace the King
Copyright © 2023 by Andy H. Niles

Tellwell Talent
www.tellwell.ca

ISBN
978-1-77941-280-5 (Hardcover)
978-1-77941-281-2 (Paperback)
978-1-77941-279-9 (eBook)

*A series of books inspired by
my beautiful daughter Savannah.*

TABLE OF CONTENTS

CHAPTER 1

HOME

The morning mist lifted, revealing the quiet village of Iron Ridge. The sunrays streamed through Horace's open window. They reflected off his shadow crystal, illuminating his entire bedroom with beautifully colored lights. *Caw! Caw! Caw!* Horace was awoken by the loud cries of a black crow perched on a tree branch just outside his window. It cried as if it was telling him to wake up.

Horace opened his eyes and rubbed them. "What's that smell?" he wondered. It smelled like burning wood. He got up and heard yelling and screaming from outside his window. Horace looked out his window towards the east and saw clouds of smoke close to his home. Moments later, Horace's mother burst into his room and shouted, "Get dressed! We have to leave!" He saw a worried look on her face and knew something was very wrong.

"Where is Dad?" Horace asked as he hurriedly got dressed by putting on his favorite leather trousers.

"Don't worry about your father right now. We must leave. He will catch up with us later."

Horace and his mother rushed out of the house as she grabbed a bag filled with supplies that she had already packed. Outside was a scene of chaos. Lots of women and children were fleeing towards the mountains in the west.

"Where are all the fathers?" Horace wondered.

As they ran to the mountains, Horace could hear loud bangs, screaming and wailing from the village behind them.

Horace did not understand what was happening as he had never seen anything like this before. Iron Ridge was a peaceful village where the men worked hard to support their families and the women were the best mothers. The men would leave for a few days and return with gifts and wealth for their families. There was never any violence.

But there was something about Iron Ridge that Horace did not know. Despite the peaceful, warm appearance, there was a deep, dark secret.

"What's going to happen to us now, Mom?" Horace asked as he gazed at his mother, who had her hands over her mouth, stifling a cry of terror. There were no men to provide for them. It seemed they were on their own, with an uncertain future.

CHAPTER 2

THE MOUNTAIN

After many hours and as the sun set, the large group of weary travelers reached halfway up Twin Mountain. They discovered a junction where the path split three ways. One continued straight between the two mountains, while the other two were left or right up each mountain. They were all tired and hungry and some of the children were crying. The group was unable to decide which way to go. Some wanted to go left, some right, and others straight. They decided to camp at the junction for the night and discuss which path to take in the morning. They agreed not to start a fire as it could attract strangers, but luckily, there was a full moon that night.

Horace and his mother decided to rest underneath a big oak tree where some other people had already fallen asleep. Horace lay on his back and gazed beyond the giant branches into the night sky; he could still hear the sobs and whispers of children in the group. They were all fearful and scared as they had never been outside of Iron Ridge. They were accustomed to having everything provided for them. Some of the people were hungry as they did not pack any food and others shared what little they had. Horace heard his stomach rumble as he, too, was hungry. He did not want to tell his mother as he tried to be a brave ten-year-old.

Suddenly, there were loud screams of terror. A few of the women and children started running aimlessly in the dark toward safety. "Wolves! Wolves! Wolves! Run for your lives!" they screamed.

Horace's mother quickly grabbed his hand. "Stay by my side and you will be okay," she told him as they ran towards the path on the left with some of the other women and children. He could hear wailing from every direction and the loud cries of people being taken down by the wolf pack.

Suddenly, Horace's mother stopped and whispered, "Don't move."

Ahead, Horace could just make out huge black shapes. They were unmoving, but Horace saw his mother trembling slightly as her grip on his arm became unbearably tight.

A cloud that had covered the moon shifted, and there, on the trail ahead of them, stood three giant wolves with shiny black fur. They were the biggest animals Horace had ever seen. He had only heard stories of wolves and that they were like dogs, except slightly bigger. But these were not slightly bigger. They were giants because they were as tall as his mother, who was the average height of an adult female.

The growling wolves glared at the small group of women and children, long white fangs clear in the light of the full moon. The wolf in the middle had some white patches on its body and was slightly bigger than the other two, with its jaws clenched and brows raised. The big wolf looked from side to side at the other two and then motioned its head forward toward Horace and his mother. The other two wolves leaned back and then pounced on the group. Horace's mother pushed him out of harm's way as the other women and children who were with them screamed.

Horace slipped and fell from his mother's push and started sliding down the hill. He tried to stop by standing and grabbing onto small trees, but instead, he began to tumble down a steep slope. He hit his head on a stump and became unconscious.

***

It was now morning, and Horace woke up in the rain. He found himself lying beside the bank of a river and did not know how he got there. He was all alone, with no one in sight.

"Hello! Hello!"

But all he could hear was his echo and the flowing water of the river, which flowed angrily as it smashed against large rocks along its path with such force, creating large slashes and white mist that filled the air. The surrounding trees were leaning over toward the river as if they wanted to bathe in it, with some branches dragging in the water. Horace did not recognize anything as he was in a strange place and the rain was pouring heavily. He knew he needed to find shelter. Horace stumbled along the riverbank in the slippery mud while struggling to maintain his balance. He was tired and hungry. He placed his hand on his head and felt a large bump.

"That must be why I have a headache," he thought. "But what happened? I don't remember anything." Horace found a big tree by the river's edge where some of the soil had eroded, exposing some of the tree's roots and what seemed like a small tunnel.

Horace got down on his hands and knees so he could place his head into the opening of the small tunnel. He could not get his shoulders inside and had to reach in with one arm and his head first by turning sideways. He eventually got both shoulders inside and straightened his legs before pulling them in. Now he was out of the rain. Inside the tunnel, it smelt like worms and rotting leaves. The ground was moist and littered with leaves and twigs. Horace could hear bugs and insects scurrying beneath the leaves as he dragged his feet to curl himself in a ball for warmth inside his small tunnel. He had heard stories of people eating grubs and insects, so he decided to try. Even though his stomach turned at the thought. Horace picked up a strange large bug with what looked like horns but decided not to eat it as it had a hard casing. It was a horned beetle. He decided to try the grubs as they were soft and looked like giant rice grains.

Horace looked at the grub in his hands before he tossed it into his mouth. He could not bear the hunger any longer. His body shivered as he took the first bite of the grub as it popped inside his mouth. He felt a milky, tangy taste that was quite different from anything he had ever eaten. Horace ate as many grubs as he could tolerate, which was just a handful because he did not like the taste. Then he tucked himself into the back of the small tunnel to try and get warm as the rain continued pouring. He felt scared as he had never been alone in the jungle before. He wondered where his mother was and why they had to leave his village.

CHAPTER 3

FRIEND

The rain had stopped, and it was around midday now. Horace wanted to find his mother and the others but did not know where to start looking. He crawled out of the tunnel and began to survey his surroundings as he could see better now. The trees were dripping wet and the air was filled with mist from the river. The sky was gray, and the air smelt fresh. Aside from the flowing river, there were sounds of frogs croaking and birds calling out as they were talking to each other. Horace began walking toward the direction that the river was flowing from, which was somewhere up the mountain. He knew the others had headed up the mountain.

He came to a section of the river where the water was calm and wide. Horace heard splashing and looked to see large fish jumping and flicking their red tails. This intrigued and amazed him, as he had never seen fish this big. Everything in the mountains seemed bigger. Horace thought it would be nice to catch one of the fish and eat it. But there was a big problem . . . he could not swim.

Horace stood there for a while and thought of how he could catch a fish. He looked around and found a long branch, which he took and broke off the protruding pieces to make a spear. While he ripped the pieces off, it tore strips of bark along the branch, which Horace then tied together to make rope. "Aahhh." Horace sighed as he looked at his new tool. His spear had a pointed edge; it was heavy enough to throw, and he had a 'rope' tied to it. Horace was ready to fish.

Horace threw his spear into the river several times with no luck. He would either throw it too early before the fish came up or too late after the fish had gone back down. Horace knew that if he were going to get one, he would have to time his throw just right. Horace waited and waited as the fish continued jumping and splashing. Then he made a really strong throw, timing it perfectly. The spear jabbed into the side of a really big fish, paralyzing it instantly. Horace hauled on his makeshift rope and could feel the weight of the enormous fish. It was heavy. He was really lucky that it was paralyzed, or it could have broken free or dragged him into the water.

Once the fish was at the riverbank, Horace struggled to lift it out of the water as he saw the enormity of its size. It was as big as himself, which was four feet long. Horace used all his strength to drag the fish onto the bank as he could not lift it. He held it by the gills and dragged it to an area where there were some large stones. He was exhausted from hauling the massive fish, so he sat and panted for a bit. Horace wondered how he was going to eat the fish as he had no fire, and everything was wet.

After resting, Horace looked around and found some flat rocks with sharp edges. He tried using them to cut the fish, but they were not sharp enough. He decided to use a rounded rock to break pieces along the edge of a sharp rock he had chosen. This made his chosen rock even sharper, like a knife. Horace tried cutting the fish with it and it worked. He cut out a piece of the tail and ate it raw. It was a bit difficult to eat at first, but he pretended it was already cooked as he screwed up his face and chewed.

Horace sliced off another piece of slimy fish and bravely carried on eating it but then felt the presence of someone or something nearby. He heard a growl. Horace slowly lifted his head and looked up to the top of the large rock in front of him. It was a wolf. It stood there with its teeth exposed all along the jawline, eyebrows raised, and poised, ready to pounce. It was smaller than the ones from his encounter last night but seemed equally as dangerous. Its fur was brilliantly white and majestic.

Horace had nowhere to go as the river was behind him and he could not swim. His heart pounded rapidly, and his breathing became heavy as he swallowed gulps of air. He looked at his spear, which was approximately six feet away, about the same distance as the wolf. He thought of jumping and grabbing his spear but knew the wolf would be too quick for him. Instead, Horace decided to inch slowly toward it, bit by bit. The wolf growled and took one step closer as Horace moved slightly. The wolf had majestic white fur, yet its face looked deadly as it snarled, exposing long fangs along its jawline. It stood about the same height as Horace, on muscular legs that were supported by paws as big as a grown man's hand and had claws as sharp as needles. There was a loud *hiss* behind Horace that made him freeze. He thought it was a snake, but this hiss sounded different. It sounded deep and as if it was protruding from large nostrils. Horace slowly turned his head and saw the largest alligator he had ever seen not too far behind him. It had massive scales that looked like armor and big teeth protruding all the way around its long, rounded snout. Horace was in serious trouble. He slowly turned his head back toward the wolf, closed his eyes, and made a big gulp as his heart pounded so hard it felt like it would burst out of his chest.

Horace felt a gust of wind above his head that came from the direction of the wolf. He opened his eyes and found that the wolf was no longer there. He turned his head again slowly toward the alligator and saw that the wolf was now between him and the alligator, facing it and growling even stronger and harder as if it dared the alligator in a challenge. The alligator hissed again, then turned and went back into the river with a flick of its massive tail.

Horace was relieved. But now he had the wolf to deal with. The wolf waited a bit until it was sure the alligator was gone, then it turned toward Horace. With glittering eyes, it looked at him and slowly walked in his direction. Horace moved to the side and was now on top of his spear. The wolf kept walking and stopped at Horace's fish, which it began to eat. It looked at Horace, whose heart was still racing as he fumbled to get hold of his spear. The wolf turned its attention back to the catch of the day and continued eating as if Horace was not even there. It ate its fill, then trotted off into the forest as its brilliant white fur disappeared in the distance.

CHAPTER 4

WHO IS THERE?

A s Horace gathered what he could salvage from the remains of the fish, he realized it was getting late in the evening, and he had not seen or heard from anyone from his village. It was getting colder, and Horace felt lonely as he really missed his mother. He knew the jungle was no place for a ten-year-old boy to be wandering around by himself. After wrapping some of the fish in broad leaf lily pads and collecting his spear and rock knife, he set off into the hills, leaving the river behind.

Horace realized he could not see the other mountain to the north and figured that he was on the south side of the southern mountain. The terrain was rugged with sharp rocks and sparse vegetation as he climbed along the face of a large cliff, being careful not to fall. But Horace eventually made his way to the top of the ridge where the other mountain was now in view. He yelled, "Hello! Hello! Hello!" But there was no reply. Only his echo in the distance. Horace noticed it was getting late and the skies were dark with rain clouds. He did not want to get caught in the rain again as it was cold at night and even colder if he got wet as he was barefoot and dressed only in tattered leather pants with no shirt.

Horace found a tree that had a thick canopy and protruding roots along the ground. He gathered lots of sticks and branches and laid them across the protruding roots to keep his bed elevated.

He remembered how his father had taught him to make a tent with tree branches and leaves, and he did exactly that. Horace's tent was almost complete. All he needed to do was add a few more branches to the top, so he looked around and found the perfect bush.

Horace did not think twice about going over to break a few branches for his tent, but suddenly, the bush began shaking, and he also heard a twig breaking. Horace froze in his tracks and stared at the bush. He did not have his spear or his makeshift knife with him. Horace found his heart was once again pounding as if it was trying to break free. He started gasping and thought of running, but where would he go? "Who's there?" he said with a trembling voice. But there was no answer.

Horace found that whatever or whomever it was, the sound of the rustling was getting closer. "Who's there!" Horace yelled. But again, there was no answer. Horace turned and ran back to his tent and grabbed his spear, holding it up, ready to throw. Then, he turned, facing the bush, and decided to hold his ground. The skies opened up and the rain started. But Horace did not move. He stood there holding his spear, watching the bush. Then came a low growl from inside the bush.

Slowly, the white head of a wolf pushed out inch by inch as it revealed itself and slowly walked toward him. There was no more growling, and it did not seem enraged. Instead, the wolf appeared calm as it came and stopped about six feet in front of Horace, who was still holding his spear.

The wolf looked at Horace, then looked at his spear. Horace stared back at the wolf and did not move a muscle. Then he noticed something as he looked deep into its golden eyes and felt humbled in its presence. It was different from the other wolves he had seen on the track with his mother. It was the same wolf from the riverside that protected him from the alligator and then ate some of his fish.

"Why was it here now? Did it come for more fish? Or did it come for me?"

CHAPTER 5

TIT FOR TAT

After a lengthy period of staring at each other, Horace was getting cold in the rain. His teeth started to chatter and his body was shivering. He decided not to attack the wolf, but it also did not attack him. Horace looked at the tent, then looked back at the wolf. He figured that if the wolf was not going to harm him, he might as well get out of the rain. Horace turned his back on the wolf, walked slowly toward his tent, and went inside, leaving his spear outside. He was wet, cold, and shivering.

The wolf did not leave, even though Horace had walked away. It walked toward the tent and stood right at the entrance with its head down, making whimpering sounds and sniffing as if it wanted to go inside but needed permission. Horace was surprised by this but still unsure of the wolf's intentions. He had his stone knife with him and could use it to defend himself if necessary. Horace looked at the wolf and said, "You can come in if you promise not to hurt me." But the wolf did not move. It just stood there whimpering. "Come inside," Horace said as he motioned with his hands. But the wolf did not move.

Horace realized the wolf was also scared, so he held out his hand toward it and said in a gentle voice, "Come in. I will not hurt you."

The wolf took slow and careful steps toward Horace's outstretched hand. Once at his hand, the wolf began to sniff, and then it started licking it with his long pink tongue. Horace felt shivers down his spine as his whole body tingled. He suddenly felt a warm feeling inside, like when his mother hugged him. Horace began rubbing the wolf's head and behind its ears as they were both experiencing a feeling of comfort and trust.

Horace's stomach made a growling sound that startled the wolf. "It's okay," said Horace. "I'm just hungry."

He reached for the fish he had packaged for his journey and began opening the lily pads. The wolf's ears perked up, its mouth opened, and its long pink tongue hung from its mouth with drool. Horace noticed the wolf was very interested in his fish and decided to share. He looked at the wolf and said, "Don't be scared. I'm going to pick up my knife now, but I won't hurt you."

Horace slowly reached for his stone knife with one hand while holding the fish in the other. The wolf watched him carefully and did not react. Horace looked back at the wolf and said, "Good boy." He began cutting the fish as he moved his stone knife back and forth until a large piece came apart.

Horace reached his hand out with a piece of the fish, offering it to the wolf, but the wolf did not move. Horace gently placed the fish on the ground and said, "Go ahead, eat it." He left it there and started to eat his piece. Again, it was a bit of a challenge for him to eat it raw, but he had no choice, even though the fish was rubbery and difficult to chew. The wolf also began eating the fish Horace had offered it, and within seconds, it was all gone. Horace looked at it and said, "You must have been really hungry," as he watched it lick its mouth with that long pink tongue from one corner all the way to the next with one smooth swoop.

After eating, Horace lay on the bedding inside his tent. Luckily, he had made it off the ground so that he was not all wet. The wolf came up beside him and lay on the bedding, too. At first, Horace was a bit frightened as his heart started beating faster, and his hands trembled. The wolf's body felt warm even though it was wet. Horace slowly placed his shaking hand around the wolf's body, ending in a warm embrace.

"This feels good," Horace thought to himself. He had never been this close to a wolf before and could hear its beating heart underneath the thick fur and huge muscles that sculpted its body. It was truly a magnificent animal and now it seemed they were friends.

CHAPTER 6

UP AND AWAY

Horace and his new friend lay together inside the tent as the rain spattered on the roof. It was dark now and Horace felt safe. He thought about his mother and what might have happened to her and the other people from his village. He knew their destination was the top of the mountain, so he would have to make his way there eventually. But Horace had a long way to go. He fell asleep beside his friend, thinking of seeing his mother and hugging her again . . hopefully soon.

Horace had slept soundly through the night, but it was morning now, and he needed to go. The wolf was not inside the tent with him as Horace opened his eyes to the sunrays. He could hear his friend growling outside as if it was about to attack someone. Horace quickly grabbed his stone knife and went out to see what the commotion was about. He could not believe his eyes. The wolf was in a defensive stance with its front paws angled with one slightly in front of the other, back hunched with its fur raised, and its tail lowered just above the ground. But that was not what made Horace's jaw drop or his eyes widen. Oh no, his reaction had nothing to do with the wolf.

Horace was looking up in complete and utter disbelief at what he saw. He had to rub his eyes a few times to check if he was seeing correctly. Horace was staring at the biggest, most gigantic snake he had ever seen or could have ever imagined. It was green and covered with black diamond patterns all over its massive body. It had a giant head with eyes as black as coal and the size of a dinner plate. Its mouth was so big that it could hold both Horace and the wolf inside it at the same time. "This must be the biggest snake in the entire world, and it is here, now, in front of me." Horace thought.

There was nothing that he or the wolf could ever do to protect themselves from this huge snake that stood as tall as Horace would if he stood on his father's shoulders. It was coiling its long and massive body as though it was getting ready to strike. Horace and the wolf would just be a tiny snack for this giant snake.

Horace realized the predicament that they were in and knew they needed to leave immediately. "Come on, boy. Let's go!" Horace shouted to the wolf. He started walking backwards and did not want to take his eyes off the giant snake. "Let's go, boy!" He yelled again to the wolf. But the wolf did not back away. Instead, it turned its head and snarled at Horace, then quickly looked back at the snake again. Horace did not stop backing away, but he also kept calling out to the wolf. He did not want to leave the friend he had just met to face whatever the snake was about to do to them.

Horace was far back enough so he could turn and run toward the mountaintop. He had no time to grab his spear and only had his stone knife. Horace frantically ran toward the bushes ahead and held his arms out in front of his head to protect himself from the branches as they slapped against his body. Horace had run for a while and was very exhausted. He started slowing down as his feet began hurting. He had cuts and bruises all over his body from running through the forest. He did not hear anything behind him, but at the same time, he did not feel safe.

"What kind of forest is this? Why are all the animals giants? Did he just lose the friend he just met?" All these thoughts were swirling in Horace's head as his feet gave way and he collapsed to the forest floor from sheer exhaustion.

CHAPTER 7

SMOKE OR CLOUD

It had been several days now since Horace last saw his wolf friend as he fled from the giant snake. But he was determined to get to the top of the mountain. Horace was sad that his wolf friend was left behind and feared he would never see him again, but he was determined to get to the top of the mountain and be reunited with his mother. He survived by eating grubs and eggs that he stole from bird nests along the way. Horace had made himself a better spear that he had chopped down using his stone knife and sharpened the tip. He even used it to catch a rabbit, but he had no fire. He wanted to enjoy the rabbit he had caught, so he was determined to start a fire and cook it.

Horace spent the day trying different ways to start a fire and was getting tired and upset. He threw his stone knife to the ground, and it fell on top of a rock and ignited orange sparks. Horace was surprised at this and tried hitting the rock again with his stone knife. Again, it sparked, and he became excited. He had found the answer to his problem. Horace was going to start a fire.

He gathered some dried tree bark and used a stone to beat it, breaking it into small shreds. He continued beating it until he had a pile of wooden strings and fibers. His father had taught him that these fibers were tinder to light a fire. Horace grabbed his stone knife and a piece of the rock and held them over the tinder. He took a deep breath, and then he struck the rocks together several times, sending a shower of orange sparks into the tinder, which burst into flames. Finally, he had done it. Horace proudly smiled at himself. Finally, he could have a cooked meal.

Horace ate his fill of the rabbit, and it was delicious. It was getting dark by now, so he decided to stay close to the fire for the night. Horace climbed a nearby tree with a big, forked branch, which he lay across and fell asleep to the sounds of crickets and birds chirping in the distance, which reminded him of being at home with his parents. He found that the forest floor was not a safe place during the night as venomous snakes and scorpions made nightly patrols in search of their preferred food—warm-blooded mammals.

In the morning, Horace's fire had gone out as he slept overnight. He climbed down from his perch, straightened his back and stretched his arms wide and tall as he yawned. He decided to make the final push to the top of the mountain as he was closer now. He made his way through the thick brush until he came to an opening where he could see the top of the mountain and a thick black cloud hovering in one spot. Horace noticed the cloud was coming from beneath the trees as there were several streams going upward.

"Clouds don't do that," Horace thought. "Could it be smoke?"

CHAPTER 8

OVER THE TOP

Finally! Horace was at the mountain plateau. It was colder there, and the air was thin. The trees looked different from the rest of the jungle as they were shorter with fat trunks and had broad leaves. The air smelt clean and fresh. But there was a familiar smell. Horace could smell burning wood in the distance. "Yes, it was definitely the smell of burning wood," Horace thought to himself. The plateau seemed far and wide, and it appeared he had a lot of ground to cover in the open to get to the location of the burning wood. "This could be dangerous," he thought.

Horace walked eagerly toward the smell as he anticipated seeing people from his village again. The sweet, ashy smell of the burning wood was getting stronger, and Horace was happy for the first time in a long time. He had been alone in the jungle, surviving all its challenges for what seemed like an eternity but was actually close to ten days now. The joy of talking to another person filled his heart. He may even see his mother.

As Horace got closer to the smoke, he began hearing muffled noises, like laughter and chattering. This was very promising. Horace was tired from his long journey to the mountaintop, but he found energy he did not know he had and started running toward the voices. It was finally over. Horace dropped everything he was carrying as he ran, even his prized stone knife. After all, he had no need for it now that he would be reunited with his people. Horace ran with his arms open wide and started shouting, "I'm here! I'm here! I made it! I'm finally here!"

Suddenly, Horace could see what looked like a hut as he got closer. But something did not seem right. Then he saw some more huts and it seemed they had started a small village. Horace was overwhelmed with joy. "Guys, I'm here! I made it!" he shouted. Then he heard a loud snap, like a branch breaking. Horace realized he had stepped on that same branch but wondered why it would make that sound as it was lying on the ground. Then he heard a lot of breaking branches as he stopped in his tracks and looked around. "Oh no!" Horace shouted as he fell into a large hole, hands clawing the air.

CHAPTER 9

MEN LIKE CHILDREN

Horace found himself at the bottom of a large hole in the ground that someone had dug and covered with branches and leaves. He had fallen into a trap. But luckily, he was unhurt. "Why would anyone make a trap this close to the settlement?" Horace wondered. They must not have expected him and perhaps it was done to stop the wolves. Horace knew he needed to get out, so he called for help. Shortly afterward, Horace heard voices approaching.

Horace looked up from the bottom of the hole. Sunlight was in his eyes, but he saw shadows of children. At least, that's what it looked like to him. He heard them speaking amongst themselves but could not understand what they were saying as it was a strange language, one that he had never heard before. They stood there for a while talking before a rope ladder was lowered into the hole for him to climb out. Horace took hold of the ladder and climbed out of the hole slowly and carefully as it swung a bit as he climbed. Once at the top, he looked down at the children standing around the hole and was surprised.

They were not children, and they were certainly not from his village. Horace was surrounded by little people—fully grown men but just a bit shorter than himself. He stood in awe as he turned around slowly, looking at them. They, too, were in awe as they stared back at him.

"Hello. My name is Horace," he said politely as he waved his hand toward them. They did not respond, but instead, they looked at each other and started talking excitedly. Again, Horace was unable to understand what they were saying.

Horace realized the men had spears and arrows with them but had laid them on the ground. They started picking up their weapons and he became concerned. The men gestured with their spears for Horace to move along as a few of them started walking in front of him. He felt they wanted him to follow but had little choice as several of them were behind him, holding spears. Horace was escorted by the small men to a hole inside a big rock with doors made from branches tied together, blocking the entrance. Then he realized it was a cage. They placed Horace inside the hole and closed it so he could not escape. Two of the men stood outside as guards with spears.

Horace sat inside the cage and thought of where his people were. He also wondered who these little people were and how they came to live at the top of the mountain. How come he had never heard of them before, not even in stories? What were they going to do with him? Was this the end? Then he said to himself, "No! I will not give up. I survived the jungle for ten days, all by myself. I am not going to give up now!"

No sooner after Horace's self-reflection, some of the small men came to his cage. But they seemed different from the ones he had first encountered. They carried spears and wore brightly colored feathers on their arms and legs with face and body paintings. One of them stepped forward, holding a coil of rope in his hand. He looked scary. His body was painted with bright colors, and he had a bone through his nose. He was only wearing a loin cloth, and his exposed skin revealed several old scars, including his face.

Before Horace could process what was happening, the cage was open, and some of the men rushed in and grabbed him. They held both his arms firmly and wrestled him out of the cage. They were really strong, as Horace's arms hurt from the sheer strength of their grip. Once outside the cage, Horace's arms and hands were bound so tightly that he could barely move them. The scary man held the other end of the rope. He looked at Horace, deep into his eyes, then turned and started walking, tugging on the rope as Horace followed, stumbling along. All the others started following behind, waving their spears and chanting loudly. To make matters worse, Horace could hear loud drumming.

CHAPTER 10

TRAGEDY

While being led by the small, strong warriors, Horace wondered how he could escape. But there were too many of them and they all had weapons. Besides, his hands were bound, and he needed them free to run. The small men led Horace away from their village down a rugged path along the far side of the plateau. There, they came to the mouth of a cave that had a lot of bones scattered at the entrance. It was decorated with skulls of different animals, but one stood out. It was the skull of a large snake. Horace's eyes bulged as it looked like the massive snake he'd seen with his friend, the wolf.

Horace was more terrified now than ever. It appeared he was going to be food for something living deep inside that dark cave. There was a stone in front of the cave that looked like an ancient tree stump with markings all over it. Horace did not understand the writings as they were in a different language. The scary man holding the rope dragged Horace over to the stump and proceeded to secure him at the base and made knots that Horace could not untie. After that, he backed away and joined the others in chanting and yelling.

It was late in the evening, and Horace watched helplessly as they danced and chanted as if they were rejoicing. Then suddenly, they divided into two groups, making a straight path from front to back. The chanting and drumming also stopped, and a loud horn bellowed, making a terrifying noise that could make the blood curdle. They all fell to their knees and bowed toward the cave entrance. Silence filled the air. Even Horace was quiet as he looked toward the entrance of the cave, heart pounding and breathing heavily, anticipating some monster coming out of the cave.

Horace waited for something to emerge from the belly of the cave. He knew there was nothing he could do now, as his bond was strong and secure. He breathed a sigh of helplessness and hung his head in defeat. But from the corner of his eye, he saw a figure approaching from the back, up the path the small people had made. He looked up and saw a man adorned in tall, decorative feathers that looked like a crown around his head. He appeared to be about the same height as Horace but more manly, with muscles and a full beard. His chest was covered with a large gold plate with the symbol of the sun and a large serpent-looking figure, or maybe it was a dragon. Horace was not quite sure.

He walked slowly up to Horace, pointed a spear at him, and yelled angrily. Horace did not understand the words, but he suspected it meant that he was out of time. He was meant to be sacrificed in a ritual he did not understand. "Why was this happening to him?" he wondered. To make matters worse, he had lost all hope as there was no one to help him. The man with the feathered crown then turned to the warriors, who were still bowed, as they knelt on the ground with heads down and arms stretched out. He raised his hands over his head while holding the spear and began chanting. The warriors all stood and began jumping and screaming and the drumming started again.

By now, the sun was setting, and Feather Crown quickly left. It seemed he was in a hurry and was shortly followed by everyone else—everyone except Horace. It seemed they were afraid of the dark, or was it of whatever was inside the cave? Nevertheless, Horace was left behind, bound to their ceremonial rock. He began whimpering as he was afraid to cry out loud. As scared as he was, he thought that the least he could do to survive was to stay silent. But it was an impossible task.

It was dark now. Horace was hungry, tired, and had no strength left in him to fight. "It won't be long now," Horace thought to himself. "This is the end."

CHAPTER 11

A JOURNEY ENDED

There was no sound from the jungle or the village of the little people. Not even the sound of crickets, beetles, or any insect. It was a dead, eerie, quiet night. Horace had stopped whimpering and was now shivering from the cold night air on the mountaintop. He was so cold his teeth started chattering. That was the only noise, and it was hard to miss. Horace tried his best to be quiet, but it was impossible.

Suddenly, a loud bellowing sound came from inside the cave. Horace's heart stopped and he found it difficult to breathe. But it was impossible for him to stop his chattering teeth. Again came the sound, but this time, it seemed to be at the mouth of the cave. Horace took one last deep breath, and within moments, he was gone. No longer bound to the ceremonial stone. No longer in front of the cave. No more chattering teeth. Now, the night was truly dead quiet. There was no more sound from the cave and the night passed without further incident.

***

The next day, the warriors from the village went back to the ceremonial site at high noon. They found exactly what they were looking for—no evidence of Horace. The rope that was used to tie Horace to the stump was severed, but there was no blood. A few of them looked at each other, puzzled. Usually, whenever they made a sacrifice, the front entrance would be covered in blood. This sacrifice seemed slightly different, but more importantly, Horace was gone. The warriors returned to their village to report their findings to their king, Feather Crown.

The king was pleased with the report from the warriors. Another successful sacrifice to the god of the cave and his people would be safe from its wrath. For years now, they'd continue the ritual, or the beast and its disciples would raid their village. Feather Crown decided it was fitting for a celebration and gave the order. This made the villagers happy. They had a great king who took care of their needs and protected them for decades.

The villagers celebrated with singing and dancing into the late evening. Everyone was happy as they were having a grand time. They all gathered at the king's court, which was a clearing, for the grand finale and had lit the fires, making the evening bright. Even the warriors who were on guard duty were there. They had nothing to fear at the time as they had traps set for trespassers and invaders, like the one that had caught Horace. Unfortunately, they did not anticipate what was about to happen.

There was a loud bellowing cry from the cave where they had made the sacrifice. This caused all the celebration and merrymaking to come to an abrupt halt. The village went quiet instantly as they listened. Again came the cry as it echoed beyond the village. Feather Crown knew there was no time to run. There was no time for the villagers to go and hide inside their huts as they were all out in the clearing.

He had done everything right, the same way he had done it for decades, and there was never a problem. What could he have done to anger the god and his disciples? Was his village now in jeopardy? Feather Crown bravely stood in front of his people with both hands raised, showing his palms and gesturing for them to be still. Only a few of the warriors had their spears and arrows with them. But he gave them directions to stand down. He did not want to anger the god any further. Within moments, Feather Crown and all the villagers were surrounded by big blue-green eyes that reflected from the fires they had lit.

There was truly nowhere for them to run.

CHAPTER 12

KING TO A GOD

There was an eerie silence among the villagers. Not even Feather Crown was moving. The big eyes slowly emerged from the darkness, revealing the beasts they belonged to . . . giant wolves. These wolves were the same ones who had attacked Horace's people at the junction several weeks ago. They were huge for Horace's people, let alone these small people.

A pack of about fifty wolves surrounded the villagers but did not attack. They did not growl or sneer. They just stood there, watching the people as if they were waiting for something. The villagers were all quiet and no one dared make a sound. Not even a baby cried or child whimpered. Feather Crown was at the front of the king's clearing, standing on his wooden platform, watching quietly. The giant wolves then retracted their front paws and seemed to bow, all at the same time, with their heads lowered and bodies curled, making their hind legs higher. Feather Crown felt a moment of pride and stood tall with his chest puffed out. Then he looked to the far end of the court and his pride became short-lived.

He quickly fell to his knees and bowed with arms stretched over his head, lowering his body and raising it over and over, all the while exclaiming, "Blaka! Blaka!" Meaning 'god of gods.' His people quickly joined him and did the same. A wolf that was smaller than the others emerged from the far end of the court. It had brilliant white fur, with beautiful golden eyes, and moved majestically and gracefully as it walked slowly toward the king.

The villagers were all fearful as no one had ever seen the queen wolf before. They had heard tales that became legends as they were told for centuries. This wolf was their god and they feared nothing more. As the white wolf walked down the center of the court, it stopped suddenly. The people gasped as they eagerly watched from a position where their heads were lowered in submission. It looked back toward the end of the court and growled. Then, a large grey wolf appeared, followed by two black ones, as if it was a parade.

The bowing king was shocked at what he saw, and so, too, were the villagers. The white wolf waited for the others to catch up and pass her, then it followed. Once at the front of the king's court, the gray wolf bowed but not to Feather Crown because on its back was precious cargo. A child. A child who was known to their god. A child who became a friend to their god. A child whom their god had fought for. Yes . . . the same child they gave as a sacrifice. Horace.

Horace dismounted the grey wolf and stood on the platform, then turned to face the wolves as they backed away slowly and stood behind the white wolf. The white wolf then howled loudly and strongly before bowing to Horace. Then it stood up and went and sat beside him. All the other wolves howled as if they were rejoicing. Horace hugged his friend, whom he missed dearly.

She was the mother of the other wolves. God to the villagers. But to her, Horace was now king. A position given to him by the god of the villagers. A position that shall not be challenged.

THE END